Research in Antarctica

Sharon Holt

NELSON
A Cengage Company

Australia • Brazil • Japan • Korea • Mexico • Singapore • Spain • United Kingdom • United States

Research in Antarctica

Text: Sharon Holt
Editor: Ben Haskin
Design: Jennifer Warwick
Series design: James Lowe
Photo researcher: Libby Henry
Production controller: Adam Bextream
Reprint: Jennifer Foo

Acknowledgements
The author and publisher would like to acknowledge permission to reproduce material from the following sources:
© Bryan & Cherry Alexander Photography: p. 8; Corbis Australia: pp. 1, 5 (inset), 7, 20, cover; Getty Images: pp. 22, 23; National Science Foundation/Calee Allen: p. 6; National Science Foundation/Josh Landis: p. 9; National Science Foundation/Peter Rejcek: p. 10; Newspix/AFP: p. 14; Photolibrary: pp. 3, 4, 5 (main), 11, 12, 13, 15, 16, 17 (both), 18, 19, 21, back cover.

Every effort has been made to trace and acknowledge copyright. However, if any infringement has occurred, the publishers tender their apologies and invite the copyright holders to contact them.

Fast Forward Independent Texts
Level 24

For product information and technology assistance,
in Australia call 1300 790 853;
in New Zealand call 0508 635 766

For permission to use material from this text or product,
please email **aust.permissions@cengage.com**

ISBN 978 0 17 017953 9
ISBN 978 0 17 017899 0 (set)

Cengage Learning Australia
Level 7, 80 Dorcas Street
South Melbourne, Victoria Australia 3205

Cengage Learning New Zealand
Unit 4B Rosedale Office Park
331 Rosedale Road, Albany, North Shore NZ 0632

For learning solutions, visit **cengage.com.au**

Printed in Australia by Ligare Pty Ltd
2 3 4 5 6 7 8 22 21 20 19 18

Sharon Holt

Contents

CHAPTER 1

Antarctica

Antarctica has an extreme environment. It is the coldest place on Earth, with the strongest winds and the driest air. The wind can change suddenly and the temperature can drop without warning.

Antarctica is often described as an untouched wilderness. It has the cleanest air in the world, and because it is so remote and isolated, very few people are able to travel there.

Scientists from around the world travel to Antarctica to study many things, including the plants and animals that live there, the **climate**, weather and astronomy. Scientists also study how life in such a difficult climate affects the people who live and work there.

emperor penguins

lichen

CHAPTER 2

Studying the Weather

Antarctica is so big that the weather on the continent affects the climate in many parts of the world. **Meteorologists** studying the weather in Antarctica have discovered a lot about climate change.

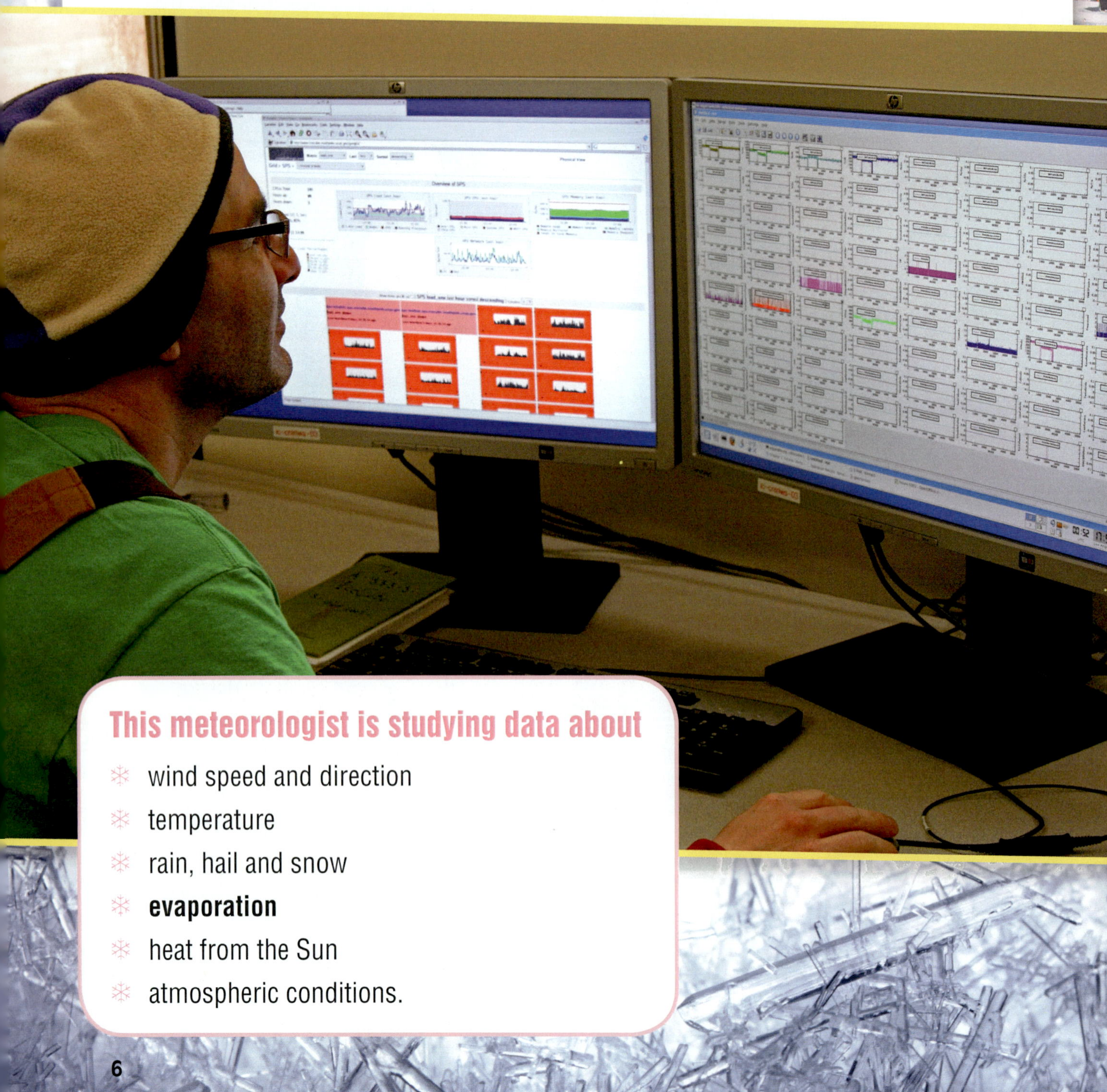

This meteorologist is studying data about

- wind speed and direction
- temperature
- rain, hail and snow
- **evaporation**
- heat from the Sun
- atmospheric conditions.

the American research base in Antarctica

Scientists in Antarctica live and work at research bases around the continent. The research bases are made up of groups of buildings run by different countries.

Automated Weather Stations

There are some parts of Antarctica where there are no research bases.

These remote places are important for weather research, so about 70 **automated** weather stations have been built to send weather data around the world by **satellite** every ten minutes.

an automated weather station

Automated weather stations are very useful because they can collect weather data in very remote areas in bad conditions. They do not need anyone to operate them, and they run on battery power. However, automated weather stations need to be repaired every three months or so, because of the extreme weather conditions in Antarctica.

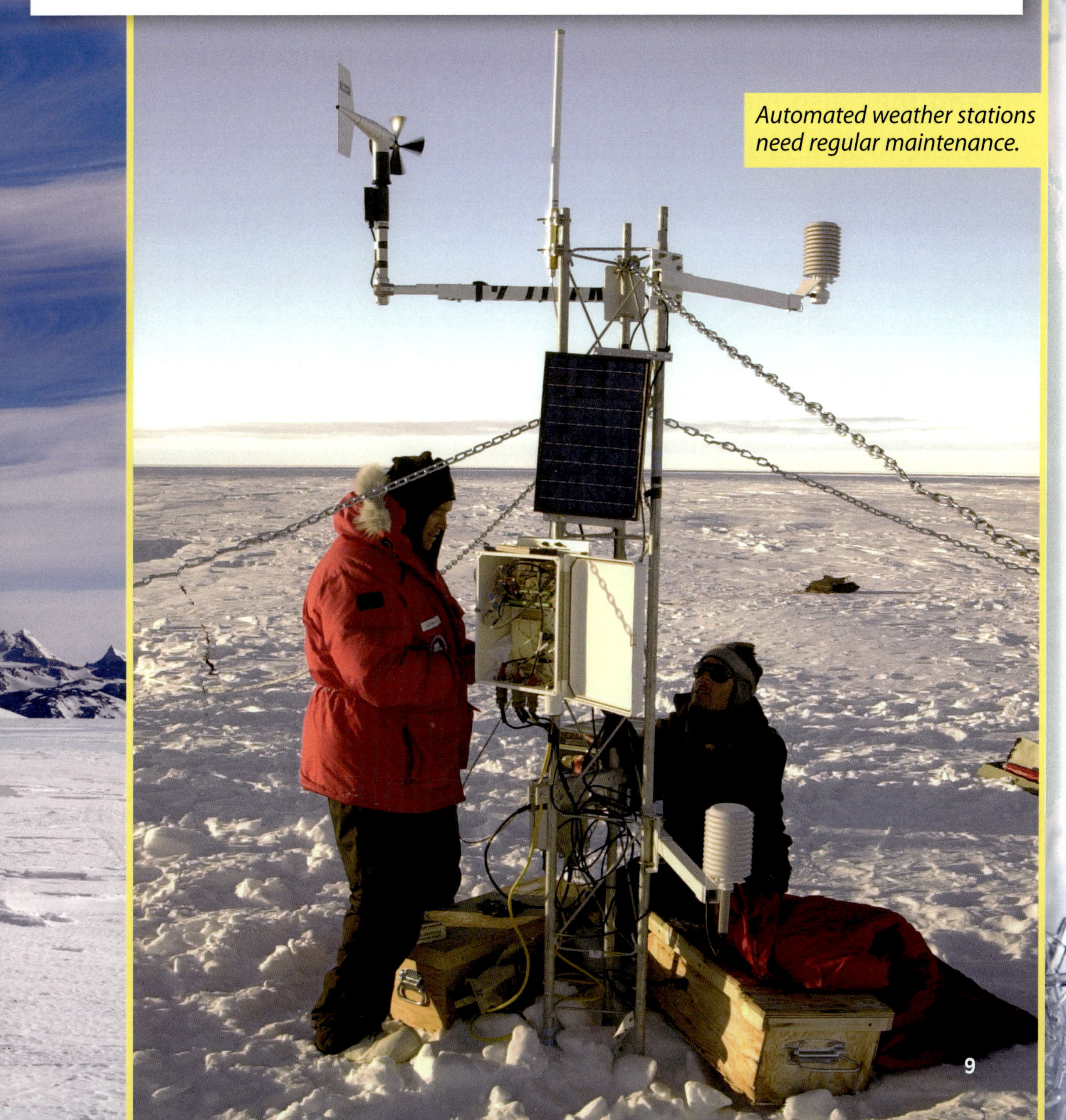

Automated weather stations need regular maintenance.

Weather Balloons

Meteorologists use special weather balloons to find out about the atmosphere. Balloons are released twice a day. They carry electronic instruments into the atmosphere and send data back to weather stations on the ground every two seconds.

The instruments carried by the balloons collect data about wind speed and direction, air pressure and temperature, and they also measure **ozone** levels. This data can be used to make local and international forecasts and to **predict** storms.

preparing equipment to attach to a weather balloon

When the balloons are released, they are about two metres wide. As they go up into the atmosphere, they expand to about six metres wide. They travel around 30 kilometres up into the atmosphere before bursting. The instruments are lost when the balloons burst.

Every day, the weather data collected around Antarctica is sent by satellite to a **United Nations** computer system in Geneva, Switzerland. Then the weather data is sent on to countries all over the world. This data helps meteorologists around the world to understand the weather patterns in their own countries.

Australian weather conditions are affected by weather systems that come from Antarctica.

Meteorologists in Antarctica even collect data to help astronauts understand the weather in space.

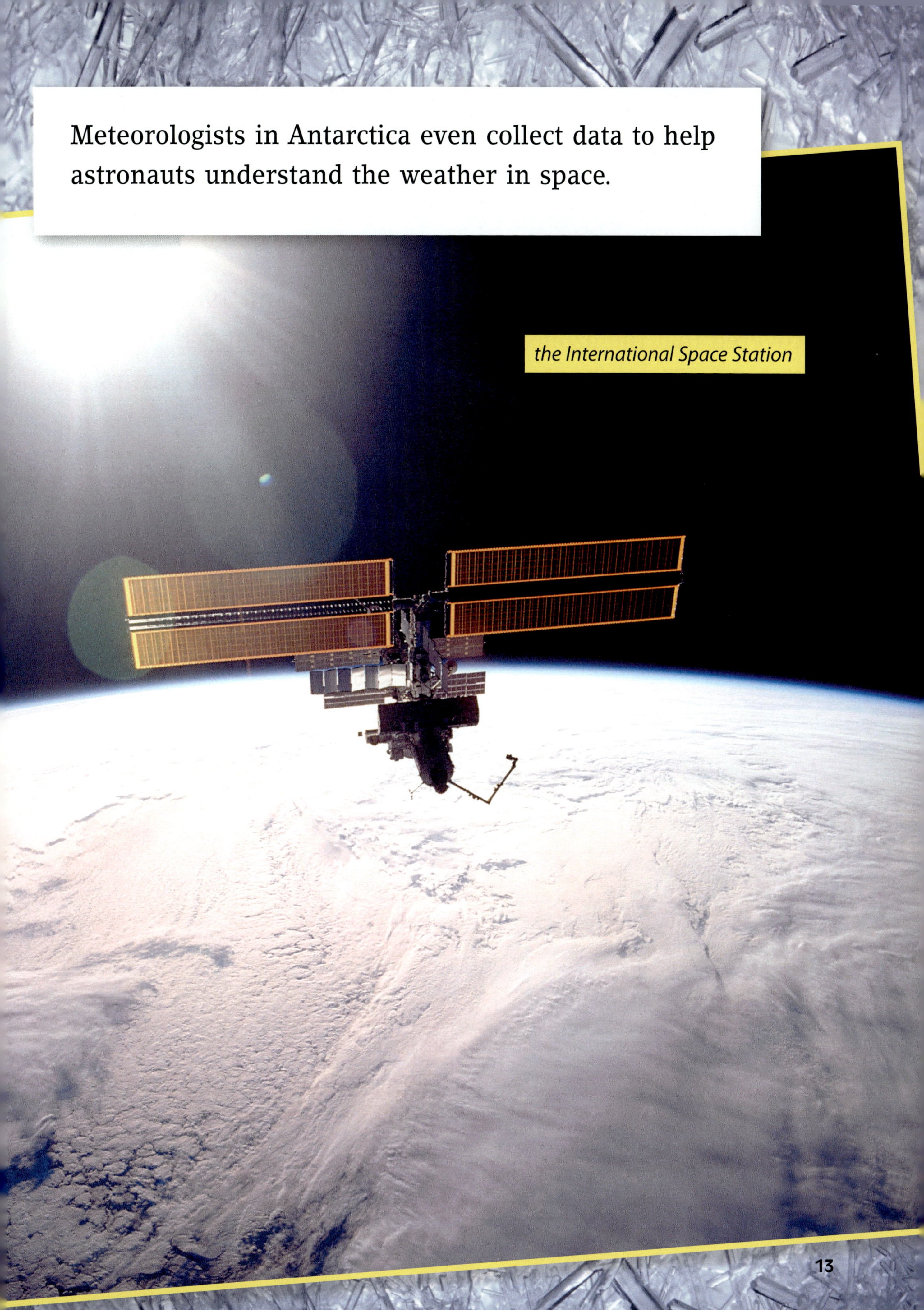

the International Space Station

CHAPTER 3

Studying the Ozone Layer

Scientists working in Antarctica in the 1970s and 1980s discovered that the ozone layer over the continent was getting thin. The ozone layer is a layer of gas high in Earth's atmosphere that protects Earth from harmful light.

Since then, they have found that global warming and problems with the ozone layer are heating the ice along Antarctica's coastline. Scientists believe that this is making the Antarctic ice break up and melt, raising sea levels around the planet and causing problems for low-lying countries.

cracks in the Wilkins Ice Shelf on the Western Antarctic Peninsula

Weather scientists in Antarctica monitor the thickness of the ozone layer year-round, using special equipment, satellite photos and weather balloons.

a scientist using an ozone measuring instrument

CHAPTER 4

Studying the Ice

Scientists in Antarctica study the ice to find out more about climate change, global warming and damage caused by greenhouse gases.

Air from the atmosphere gets trapped in the ice and stays there for thousands of years. Scientists believe some of the ice in Antarctica is up to 100 000 years old.

Scientists drill deep into the ice to collect long tubes of old ice. They work out how old the layers in the ice tubes are. Then they **analyse** the air bubbles trapped in the different layers to find out about changes in the climate and atmosphere over thousands of years.

air bubbles trapped in ice

cutting up an ice core sample

Scientists study the levels of oxygen and hydrogen gas trapped in the frozen air bubbles. They also look at the levels of greenhouse gases such as carbon dioxide. Using these studies, scientists have learned that there is twice as much carbon dioxide in the atmosphere now than there was 250 years ago.

Burning fossil fuels releases carbon dioxide into the air.

a scientist studying ice samples

By studying the ice, scientists can learn about how the climate has changed over many years and better understand the relationship between the amount of carbon dioxide in the atmosphere and Earth's temperature. This helps them to measure the impact humans have had on Earth, and to understand how Earth's climate may keep changing in years to come.

CHAPTER 5

Research in the Future

Antarctica is like a huge scientific weather laboratory that gives us data about the weather in the past, the present and the future.

Today, scientists in Antarctica are spending a lot of time researching the effects of global climate change. Ice scientists study the impact of rising water and air temperatures on the Antarctic ice sheets. They use this data to model future sea-level rises around the world.

scientists studying Antarctic ice

Scientists predict that if very large pieces break off the ice sheets and melt, sea levels around the world may rise by up to 88 centimetres by 2100. This would mean that many low-lying areas around the world would be flooded, and millions of people who live in coastal areas would be affected. Sea levels around the world have already begun to rise.

Sea water often floods Jakarta, Indonesia. This is happening more often as sea levels rise.

The research done in Antarctica is of great value to many countries and organisations including the United Nations. Governments and organisations around the world are using the research to address the climate change problem for the future.

Glossary

analyse to closely study something

automated a thing that works by itself

climate the type of weather that a place usually has

evaporation the change from liquid to gas, without boiling

meteorologists scientists who study the weather

ozone a gas that stops some harmful ultraviolet sunlight from getting to Earth

predict to say what will happen in the future

satellite a machine that orbits Earth, used for communication and to take photographs of Earth from space

United Nations an association of nations that promotes international peace and cooperation

Index